PREHISTORIC MAMMALS

Consulting Editor: Carl Mehling

Skyview Books
an imprint of
WINDMILL BOOKS
New York

Published in 2010 by Windmill Books, LLC
303 Park Avenue South, Suite # 1280, New York, NY 10010-3657

CREDITS:
Consulting Editor: Carl Mehling
Designer: Graham Beehag

Publisher Cataloging in Publication

Prehistoric mammals / consulting editor, Carl Mehling.
    p. cm. – (Discovering dinosaurs)
Summary: With the help of fossil evidence this book provides physical descriptions of twenty-nine prehistoric mammals.—Contents: Borhyena—Platybeladon—Thylacosmilus—Coryphodon—Hyracotherium—Mesonyx—Uintatherium—Andrewsarchus—Brontotherium—Arsinoitherium—Pyrotherium—Palaeocastor—Amebelodon—Daeodon (Dinohyus)—Deinogalerix—Homalodotherium—Moropus—Borophagus—Syndyoceras—Megatherium—Sivatherium—Doedicurus—Smilodon—
Woolly Mammoth—Homotherium—Coelodonta—Diprotodon—Glyptodon—Megaloceros.
ISBN 978-1-60754-779-2. – ISBN 978-1-60754-787-7 (pbk.)
ISBN 978-1-60754-861-4 (6-pack)
1.   Mammals, Fossil—Juvenile literature   [1. Mammals, Fossil
2. Prehistoric animals]   I. Mehling, Carl   II. Series
569—dc22

Printed in the United States

CPSIA Compliance Information: Batch #BW10W: For further information contact Windmill Books, New York, New York at 1-866-478-0556.

CONTENTS

Introduction

Imagining what our world was like in the distant past is a lot like being a detective. There were no cameras around, and there were no humans writing history books. In many cases, fossils are all that remain of animals who have been extinct for millions of years.

Fossils are the starting point that scientists use to make educated guesses about what life was like in prehistoric times. And while fossils are important, even the best fossil can't tell the whole story. If snakes were extinct, and all we had left were their bones, would anyone guess that they could snatch bats from the air in pitch-black caves? Probably not, but there is a Cuban species of snake that can do just that. Looking at a human skeleton wouldn't tell you how many friends that person had, or what their favorite color was. Likewise, fossils can give us an idea of how an animal moved and what kind of food it ate, but they can't tell us everything about an animal's behavior or what life was like for them.

Our knowledge of prehistoric life is constantly changing to fit the new evidence we have. While we may never know everything, the important thing is that we continue to learn and discover. Learning about the history of life on Earth, and trying to piece together the puzzle of the dinosaurs, can help us understand more about our past and future.

Borhyaena

• ORDER • Sparassodonta • FAMILY • Borhyaenidae • GENUS & SPECIES • *Borhyaena macrodenta, B. tuberata*

VITAL STATISTICS

FOSSIL LOCATION	South America
DIET	Carnivorous
PRONUNCIATION	Bore-high-EE-nuh
WEIGHT	220 lb (100 kg)
LENGTH	5ft (1.5 m)
HEIGHT	Unknown
MEANING OF NAME	"Devouring hyena" because it was probably very fierce and was similar to hyenas

FOSSIL EVIDENCE

Fossils of the hyena-like *Borhyaena* were found in the early rocks from the Miocene era in what is now Argentina. Like many fierce carnivores, the *Borhyaena* skull was large and its teeth were heavy, broad, and did a good job of crushing its prey, although its fangs were not particularly long. *Borhyaena* was probably not a fast mover. It may have ambushed prey from behind cover, grasping its victims in its claws.

PREHISTORIC ANIMAL

NEOGENE

Borhyaena was a marsupial — a mammal that carries its young in a pouch. It was heavily built and probably could not run very fast on its flat feet and short legs.

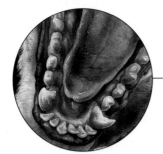

TEETH
The teeth were heavy and broad and possibly strong enough to crush bone.

Borhyaena was found in what is now Argentina in South America.

HOW BIG IS IT?

FEET
The four claws on each of *Borhyaena's* feet made it a strong predator.

TIMELINE (millions of years ago)

540	505	438	408	360	280	248	208	146	65	1.8 to today

Platybelodon

VITAL STATISTICS

FOSSIL LOCATION	Worldwide
DIET	Herbivorous
PRONUNCIATION	Platty-BELL-oh-don
WEIGHT	3.9 tons (4000 kg)
LENGTH	20 ft (6 m)
HEIGHT	9 ft (2.8 m) at the shoulder
MEANING OF NAME	Possibly "broad point tooth" (or broad tusk) for its flat lower tusks

WHERE IN THE WORLD?

Platybelodon fossils have been found worldwide.

Platybelodon, which lived around 15 million years ago, was related to the modern elephant. *Platybelodon* lived in swampy savannahs and prairies and likely ate soft leaves and tree bark.

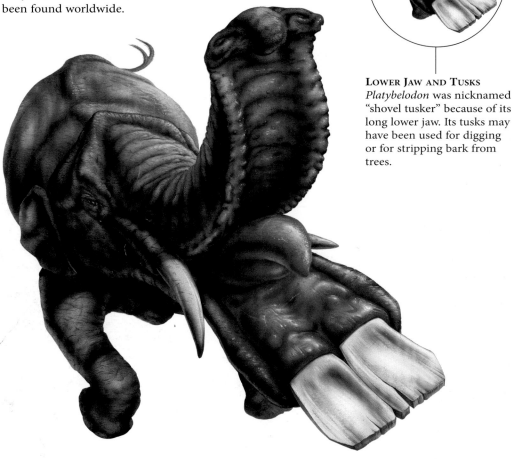

LOWER JAW AND TUSKS
Platybelodon was nicknamed "shovel tusker" because of its long lower jaw. Its tusks may have been used for digging or for stripping bark from trees.

FOSSIL EVIDENCE

Platybelodon may have crossed the land bridge between northwest North America and eastern Siberia, leaving its fossils in both areas. Its huge lower jaw had two flat teeth at the front. It had teeth in its cheeks to grind up leaves before swallowing them. *Platybelodon* also had two sharp, downward-facing tusks. These might have been used to strip the bark off trees for food, to dig for water when the ground was dry, or as weapons.

TEETH
Platybelodon's teeth and the wear patterns on its teeth and tusks show that it could eat many different types of plants.

HOW BIG IS IT?

PREHISTORIC ANIMAL

NEOGENE

TIMELINE (millions of years ago)

540	505	438	408	360	280	248	208	146	65	1.8 to today

Thylacosmilus

• ORDER • Sparassodonta • FAMILY • Thylacosmilidae • GENUS & SPECIES • *Thylacosmilus atrox, T. lentis*

VITAL STATISTICS

FOSSIL LOCATION	South America
DIET	Carnivorous
PRONUNCIATION	thigh-LAK-o-SMY-lus
WEIGHT	200 lb (90 kg)
LENGTH	8 ft (2.5 m)
HEIGHT	2 ft (0.6 m)
MEANING OF NAME	"Pouch saber" (pouched mammal with saber teeth)

Thylacosmilus was a lot like the saber-toothed cats, except for two big differences. It was a marsupial and it lived in South America.

Thylacosmilus's fangs look very much like those of a saber-toothed cat, but so does the whole body of the animal. This is because the two animals led lives that were very much alike. One big difference, though, would have been the marsupium, or brood pouch, used to raise the young of the species.

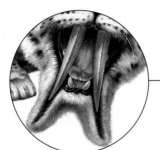

FANGS
The sabers (fangs) of some meat-eating carnivores are usually thought to be for stabbing, but those of *Thylacosmilus* might not have been strong enough for that.

WHERE IN THE WORLD?

Most *Thylacosmilus* fossils have been found in Argentina; a few have been found at other locations in South America.

FOSSIL EVIDENCE

Most of what we know about *Thylacosmilus* comes from two partial skeletons found in Pliocene deposits in Argentina. But other specimens, also incomplete, show that it lived from at least the late Miocene and on into the Pleistocene until about two million years ago. Land carnivores are usually more rare than herbivores and fewer specimens of *Thylacosmilus* are expected in the fossil record than of their prey. Because they did not have retractable claws, we know that they hunted very differently than modern cats. All cats, except the cheetah, have retractable claws, which helps keep them sharp.

PREHISTORIC ANIMAL

NEOGENE

HOW BIG IS IT?

EXTINCTION
Thylacosmilus and many other South American marsupials disappeared during the Pleistocene, around the same time that many animals were moving between North and South America.

TIMELINE (millions of years ago)

| 540 | 505 | 438 | 408 | 360 | 280 | 248 | 208 | 146 | 65 | 1.8 to today |

Coryphodon

• **ORDER** • Pantodonta • **FAMILY** • Coryphodontidae
• **GENUS & SPECIES** • Several species within the genus *Coryphodon*

VITAL STATISTICS

FOSSIL LOCATION	Europe, North America
DIET	Herbivorous
PRONUNCIATION	Cor-ee-FOE-don
WEIGHT	1102 lb (500 kg)
LENGTH	7ft 6 in (2.25 m)
HEIGHT	3ft 4in (1 m) at the shoulder
MEANING OF NAME	Possibly "point tooth" for the pointed tooth ridges

WHERE IN THE WORLD?

Coryphodon was found in Europe and in North Dakota.

Coryphodon **lived in swamps and marshes 55 million years ago. It is the largest mammal that we know of from its time, with long forelimbs and short back legs, which were needed to support its weight.**

TUSKS
Coryphodon's tiny tusks, which were probably only on the male of the species, were used to pull up plants in the marshes.

FOSSIL EVIDENCE

Coryphodon was an early mammal that lived in the early Eocene epoch around 55 million years ago. Like the modern hippopotamus (to whom it is not closely related,) *Coryphodon* lived in marshes, which means it spent time on land and in shallow waters. It was somewhere between the size of a modern tapir and a rhinoceros. *Coryphodon* was not one of the more intelligent early mammals — paleontologists have estimated that its brain-to-bodyweight ratio was 1 lb 3 oz (90 g) to 1102 lb (500 kg).

PREHISTORIC ANIMAL

TERTIARY (EOCENE)

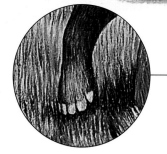

FEET
Each foot ended in five toes that look like a modern elephant's. Each toe ended in a small hoof.

HOW BIG IS IT?

TIMELINE (millions of years ago)

540	505	438	408	360	280	248	208	146	65	1.8 to today

Hyracotherium

• **ORDER** • Perissodactyla • **FAMILY** • Palaeotheriidae • **GENUS & SPECIES** • *Hyracotherium leporinum*

VITAL STATISTICS

FOSSIL LOCATION	Europe, North America
DIET	Herbivorous
PRONUNCIATION	High-rah-co-THEER-ium
WEIGHT	15 lb (6.8 kg)
LENGTH	2 ft (60 cm)
HEIGHT	9 in (23 cm) at the shoulder
MEANING OF NAME	"Hyrax beast" because it may have looked like a hyrax

WHERE IN THE WORLD?

Fossils have been found in England and in Utah.

Hyracotherium, which lived around 50 million years ago, was once thought to be the earliest-known horse, but it is now considered a paleothere— a group closely related to horses.

FACE
Hyracotherium's face looked a lot like the faces of modern Arabian horses. It also had a diastema (space) between its front and back teeth.

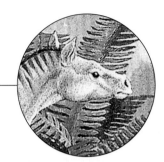

FOSSIL EVIDENCE

The first *Hyracotherium* fossils were found in England in 1841 by the paleontologist Richard Owen. The discovery was not a complete skeleton, and Owen called it "a hyrax-like beast." The hyrax is a small, modern mammal that eats plants. In 1876, the American paleontologist Othniel C. Marsh found a complete skeleton, which he named *Eohippus* (meaning "dawn horse.") However, *Hyracotherium* is the correct name. The skeleton had four toes, with hooves on each of the front feet and three toes with hooves on each back foot. *Hyracotherium* had a long skull and 44 teeth.

PREHISTORIC ANIMAL

TERTIARY (EOCENE)

HOW BIG IS IT?

BODY SIZE
Although *Hyracotherium* was an early relative of much larger animals including the rhinoceros, it was only the size of a small dog.

TIMELINE (millions of years ago)

540	505	438	408	360	280	248	208	146	65	1.8 to today

Mesonyx

• **ORDER** • Mesonychia • **FAMILY** • Mesonychidae • **GENUS & SPECIES** • *Mesonyx obtusidens, M. uintensis*

VITAL STATISTICS

FOSSIL LOCATION	North America, east Asia
DIET	Carnivorous
PRONUNCIATION	Mez-ON-icks
WEIGHT	Unknown
LENGTH	8 ft (2.5 m)
HEIGHT	Unknown
MEANING OF NAME	"Middle claw"

FOSSIL EVIDENCE

Paleontologists discovered *Mesonyx uintensis,* one of the two officially recognized species, in Wyoming. They found fossils from the Upper Eocene era in northern Utah that were 45 million years old. From the fossils they unearthed, they calculated that *Mesonyx's* face measured 8 in (20.6 cm) in length and that its skull was 17 in (43 cm) long. This was the skull of a predator; *Mesonyx* had a large sagittal crest above its braincase, which held powerful jaw muscles and caused a strong bite.

PREHISTORIC ANIMAL

TERTIARY (EOCENE)

Mesonyx was a wolflike mammal that probably lived by the sea around 45 million years ago.

PREDATOR ORIGINS
Mesonyx was a mesonychid, a family of predators that is sometimes called by its older name Acreodi, which first appeared around 50 million years ago.

WHERE IN THE WORLD?

Mesonyx was found in Wyoming and northern Utah, and in east Asia.

FEET
Mesonyx probably hunted hoofed plant eaters and probably moved very fast.

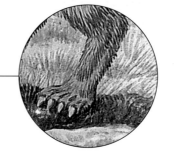

HOW BIG IS IT?

TIMELINE (millions of years ago)

540	505	438	408	360	280	248	208	146	65	1.8 to today

Uintatherium

• **ORDER** • Dinocerata • **FAMILY** • Uintatheriidae • **GENUS & SPECIES** • *Uintatherium anceps*

VITAL STATISTICS

FOSSIL LOCATION	United States
DIET	Herbivorous
PRONUNCIATION	You-in-ta-THER-ium
WEIGHT	6000 lb (2721 kg)
LENGTH	15 ft (4.5 m)
HEIGHT	5 ft (1.5 m)
MEANING OF NAME	"Uinta beast" for the Uinta Basin in Utah, where the fossils were found

Uintatherium was a mammal that looked a lot like the modern rhinoceros. It lived 45 million years ago and its family, the Uintatheriidae, had skulls unlike any other group of mammals.

OSSICONES
Uintatherium had three pairs of bony ossicones on its head. The function of these is unknown; they could have been for defense or for mating rituals just like the ossicones that giraffes have.

WHERE IN THE WORLD?

Fossils have been found in Wyoming.

FOSSIL EVIDENCE

Uintatherium fossils have been discovered near Fort Bridger in Wyoming. Six individuals, which were probably males, were found with skulls that had six large bony knobs in the front. The skulls were very heavy because of the thick bone walls. As with the modern elephant, the skulls were a little lighter because of hollow spaces in the bone. Some scientists believe that *Uintatherium* rarely strayed far from rivers or lakes, where it fed on marsh plan[ts] other water[...]

Andrewsarchus

VITAL STATISTICS

FOSSIL LOCATION	Mongolia
DIET	Possibly omnivorous
PRONUNCIATION	AN-droo-SAR-kus
LENGTH	2.7 ft (83 cm) (skull)
LENGTH	13 ft (4 m) (body)
HEIGHT	Unknown
MEANING OF NAME	"Andrews' chief," named for expedition leader Roy Chapman Andrews

FOSSIL EVIDENCE

A single skull without lower jaws is all that is known of *Andrewsarchus*. It was discovered in the early 1920s, and later expeditions to the area of the find have failed to reveal any more specimens of this animal. The skull is well preserved though, and almost complete, showing huge

Andrewsarchus had a very big skull and enormous jaw muscles for a powerful bite. But it also had relatively small eyes and blunt teeth, which suggest that it might not have been an active hunter. This leaves paleontologists wondering whether *Andrewsarchus* was the largest meat-eating mammal of all time, or a plant-eater. If its body was similar to its relatives, it walked on hooved feet instead of the claws expected for a carnivore.

TEETH
The powerful bite and blunt teeth suggest that *Andrewsarchus* was able to crush large bones and so might have been a scavenger.

• **ORDER** • Mesonychia • **FAMILY** • Triisodontidae • **GENUS & SPECIES** • *Andrewsarchus mongoliensis*

WHERE IN THE WORLD?

Fossils have been found in Irdin Manha (also spelled Erdeni-Mandal), in the Gobi Desert, Mongolia.

EYES
The eyes were small and set low on the skull, close to the rear of the tooth row.

DID YOU KNOW?
Andrewsarchus was once thought to be a close relative to the ancestor of whales. More recent work has shown that they are not as closely related as we first thought.

TIMELINE (millions of years ago)

540	505	438	408	360	280	248	208	146	65	1.8 to today

Brontotherium

VITAL STATISTICS

FOSSIL LOCATION	North America
DIET	Herbivorous
PRONUNCIATION	Bron-toth-EE-rium
WEIGHT	1.76 tons (1.8 tonnes)
LENGTH	Unknown
HEIGHT	8 ft (2.5 m) at the shoulder
MEANING OF NAME	"Thunder beast" for its great size and to honor the legends of the Sioux Native Americans on whose lands it was first found

FOSSIL EVIDENCE

Brontotherium is well known from many well preserved skeletons. Their most striking feature is the flattened, forked nasal horns whose purpose is unknown. Because of the range of features and sizes of the skulls, several species have been assigned to this genus, but it seems that there are much fewer species than first thought. In fact, some recent research proposes that *Brontotherium* should actually be put in the brontothere genus *Megacerops*.

PREHISTORIC ANIMAL

TERTIARY (EOCENE)

Brontotherium looks a lot like the modern rhinoceros and, as the meaning of its name suggests, it probably shook the ground when on the move. The first discoverers of *Brontotherium* were probably Native American Sioux who found their skeletons after rainstorms had washed away soil. The Sioux believed that the noise these creatures made occurred when they were running across the clouds, which was why they called *Brontotherium* "thunder horse." Paleontologists have suggested that the *Brontotherium* specimens that the Sioux found had all died together as a result of volcanic eruptions.

SKULL
Brontotherium's huge skull was held up by powerful neck muscles, which were supported by the very long spine.

HOW BIG IS IT?

LOCAL DANGERS

Brontotherium roamed across a large part of North America around 56 million years ago, but it was a dangerous place to be. In addition to rainstorms and drought, there was another even bigger danger. Frequent volcanic eruptions occurred as the Rocky Mountains were being formed, and these had the power to kill entire herds of *Brontotherium* at once.

• **ORDER** • Perissodactyla • **FAMILY** • Brontotheriidae • **GENUS & SPECIES** • Several species within the genus *Brontotherium*

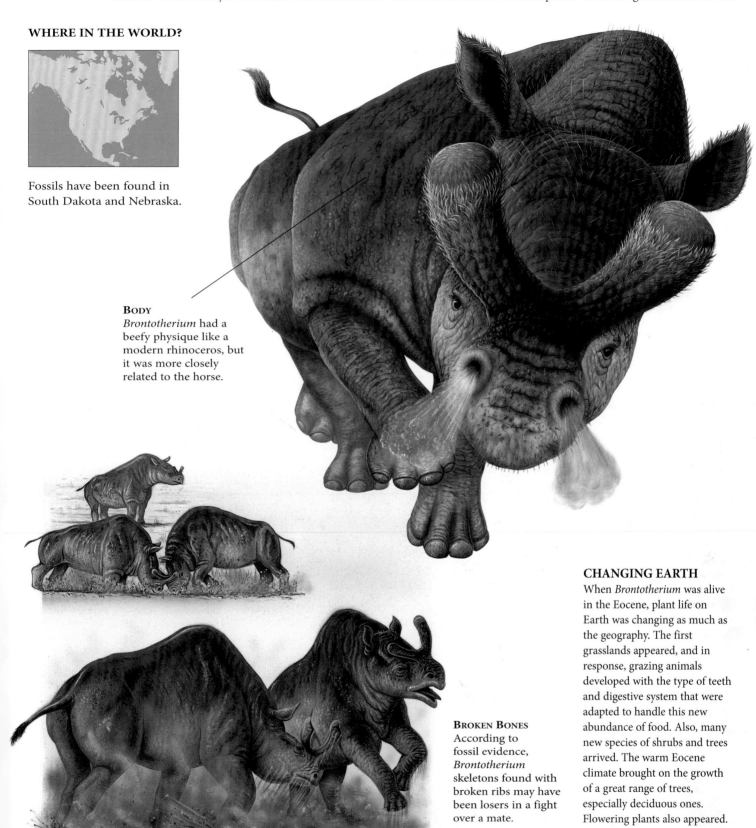

WHERE IN THE WORLD?

Fossils have been found in South Dakota and Nebraska.

BODY
Brontotherium had a beefy physique like a modern rhinoceros, but it was more closely related to the horse.

BROKEN BONES
According to fossil evidence, *Brontotherium* skeletons found with broken ribs may have been losers in a fight over a mate.

CHANGING EARTH

When *Brontotherium* was alive in the Eocene, plant life on Earth was changing as much as the geography. The first grasslands appeared, and in response, grazing animals developed with the type of teeth and digestive system that were adapted to handle this new abundance of food. Also, many new species of shrubs and trees arrived. The warm Eocene climate brought on the growth of a great range of trees, especially deciduous ones. Flowering plants also appeared.

TIMELINE (millions of years ago)

| 540 | 505 | 438 | 408 | 360 | 280 | 248 | 208 | 146 | 65 | 1.8 to today |

Brontotherium

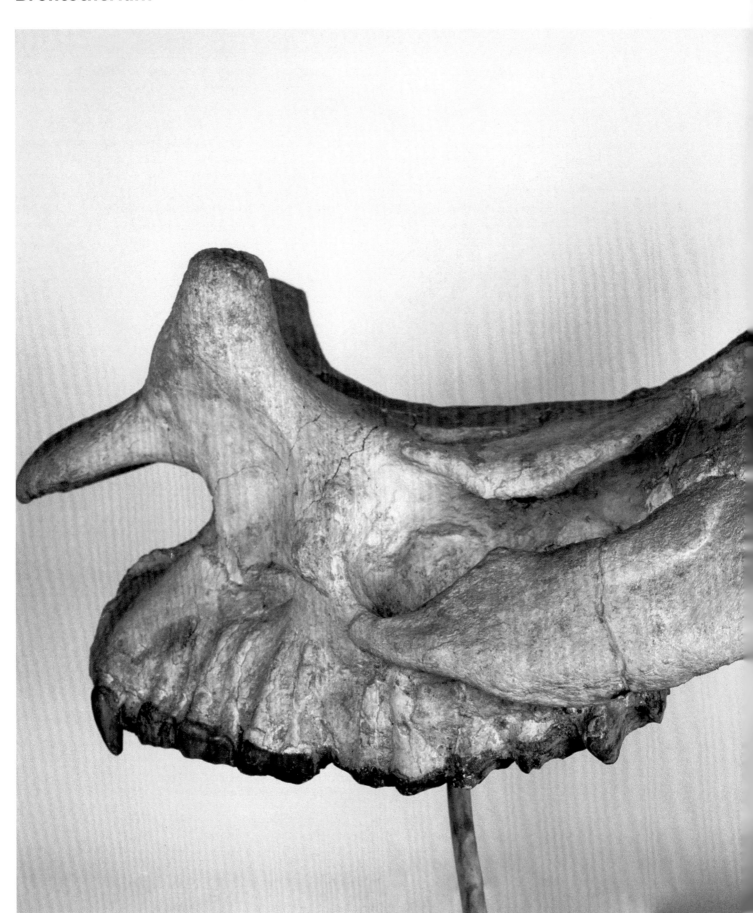

• **ORDER** • Perissodactyla • **FAMILY** • Brontotheriidae • **GENUS & SPECIES** • Several species within the genus *Brontotherium*

EOCENE CHANGES

The Eocene was a period that saw many fast changes in the geography of Earth. *Brontotherium* lived in the later part of the Eocene, which lasted until around 38 million years ago. Around this time, its North American habitat, the Great Valley of California, sank below the Pacific Ocean together with a large area of the Atlantic and the coastal plain of the Gulf of Mexico. The area of underwater coastal plain stretched from New Jersey to Texas, into the Mississippi River valley and north as far as southern Illinois. A large piece of *Brontotherium*'s home territory therefore disappeared at this time. In other parts of the world, there were many changes as well. The Eocene Epoch saw the Norwegian and Greenland Seas opening up. In southern Europe, North Africa, and southwest Asia, most of the land was covered by the Mediterranean Sea. The Eocene climate was pleasantly warm. The "new" Eocene mammals were the ancestors (early relatives) of animals familiar today, including the rhinoceros, tapir, camel, pig, rat and other rodents, the monkey, and the whale.

Arsinoitherium

• ORDER • Embrithopoda **• FAMILY •** Arsinoitheriidae
• GENUS & SPECIES • Several species within the genus *Arsinoitherium*

VITAL STATISTICS

Fossil Location	Africa and Middle East
Diet	Herbivorous
Pronunciation	ar-sin-OH-ih-THEE-ree-um
Weight	Unknown
Length	10 ft (3 m)
Height	5 ft 10 in (1.8 m) at the shoulder
Meaning of name	Named after the third-century CE Egyptian Queen, Arsinoe II, whose palace at Fayyum was close to the site where its fossils were discovered

FOSSIL EVIDENCE

Complete *Arsinoitherium* skeletons have been found only in Egypt. Pieces of the jaws of its relatives were discovered in southeastern Europe and Mongolia and seem to be of an earlier date than the Egyptian finds. The fossils found in Ethiopia in 2003 were around 27 million years old. *Arsinoitherium*'s most interesting features were the two huge horns that stuck up just above its nose. By contrast, the two knob-shaped horns directly behind them were tiny. *Arsinoitherium* seems to have spent most of the day feeding to maintain its hefty physique.

PREHISTORIC ANIMAL

TERTIARY (OLIGOCENE)

WHERE IN THE WORLD?

Fossils have been found in Fayyum in Egypt, Mongolia, Turkey, and Ethiopia.

Arsinoitherium, which looks like the modern rhinoceros, lived in the tropical rain forest at the edge of swamps around 36 million years ago. Strongly built and hefty, *Arsinoitherium*'s size usually made it safe from predators.

HORNS
Two huge horns made of bone stuck out like knives from just above the nose.

LEGS AND FEET
Arsinoitherium spent most of its time in the water. Its broad flat feet and long legs were better adapted for wading and swimming than walking.

HOW BIG IS IT?

TIMELINE (millions of years ago)

540	505	438	408	360	280	248	208	146	65	1.8 to today

Pyrotherium

VITAL STATISTICS

FOSSIL LOCATION	Argentina, Bolivia
DIET	Herbivorous
PRONUNCIATION	Pie-ro-THEE-rium
WEIGHT	Unknown
LENGTH	10 ft (3 m)
HEIGHT	5 ft (1.5 m)
MEANING OF NAME	"Fire beast" because it was first found in an ancient volcanic ashfall

FOSSIL EVIDENCE

Pyrotherium was an ungulate (an animal with hooves) and looked like the modern elephant except for its trunk, which was probably shorter. Like the elephant, *Pyrotherium* had thick, sturdy legs to support its heavy weight.
Pyrotherium lived from the early Oligocene in Argentina to the late Oligocene when it left its fossils at Salla in Bolivia. When *Pyrotherium* lived in the early Oligocene, some of the first grasslands, elephants, and the first horses were on the scene.

PREHISTORIC ANIMAL

TERTIARY (OLIGOCENE)

Pyrotherium lived in Argentina around 34 million years ago. It was named "fire beast" because the site where it was found was covered by ash from an ancient volcanic eruption.

DID YOU KNOW?
Pyrotherium looks like a modern elephant, but that is because they developed in similar environments, not because they are closely related.

WHERE IN THE WORLD?

Fossils have been found in Bolivia and Argentina in South America.

HOW BIG IS IT?

JAW
There were two flat, forward-facing tusks on the upper jaw and two on the lower jaw.

TIMELINE (millions of years ago)

540	505	438	408	360	280	248	208	146	65	1.8 to today

Palaeocastor

• **ORDER** • Rodentia • **FAMILY** • Castoridae • **GENUS & SPECIES** • Several species within the genus *Palaeocastor*

VITAL STATISTICS

Fossil Location	United States
Diet	Herbivorous
Pronunciation	Pal-aye-oh-CASS-tor
Weight	Unknown
Length	8 in (20 cm)
Height	Unknown
Meaning of name	"Prehistoric beaver"

FOSSIL EVIDENCE

The fossilized burrows of *Palaeocastor*, known as *Daemonelix* (devil's corkscrews,) were found in 1891 in Nebraska, although the mammal itself had first been described in 1869. Fossil evidence suggests that *Palaeocastor* may have lived in family groups like modern beavers, though they were mainly burrowing, and did not live in the water. In 1977, surface markings on a fossilized burrow allowed paleontologists to understand how it made its burrows. The burrows had been a mystery until the fossilized body of a prehistoric beaver was discovered in one of them. Until then, it had been thought that they were the fossilized roots of a plant.

PREHISTORIC ANIMAL

TERTIARY (MIOCENE)

Palaeocastor was a burrowing animal that fossil evidence suggests lived in family groups. Their burrows were shaped like corkscrews. They dug them with their teeth, and not with their claws.

TEETH
At first scientists thought that *Palaeocaster* dug burrows with its feet, but later study showed that it used its strong incisors.

TAIL
Since it lived on land, *Palaeocaster*'s tail was not flattened like the swimming tail of modern beavers.

HOW BIG IS IT?

WHERE IN THE WORLD?

Remains have been found in North and South Dakota and in Harrison, Nebraska.

TIMELINE (millions of years ago)

540	505	438	408	360	280	248	208	146	65	1.8 to today

Amebelodon

VITAL STATISTICS

Fossil Location	United States, eastern China, North Africa
Diet	Herbivorous
Pronunciation	Am-eh-BELL-oh-don
Weight	22,000 lb (10,000 kg)
Length	Unknown
Height	8 ft (2.4 m)
Meaning of name	Possibly "together point tooth" (or "fused tusk") because of its shovel-like lower tusks

FOSSIL EVIDENCE

Amebelodons belonged to a group called gomphotheres. Although *Amebelodon* was nicknamed a "shovel tusker" and used its lower tusks to shovel food into its mouth, it has been suggested that the tusks had more uses than this. For example, they could have been used to strip the bark off of trees, a function that some paleontologists think is confirmed by the wear patterns they have. In addition, the short flap-shaped trunk shown in many *Amebelodon* illustrations may wrong— some scientists now think that it had a long trunk like a modern elephant's.

Amebelodon was the relative of the mammoth and the modern elephant. Appearing first in North America, *Amebelodon* migrated to China across the landbridge now covered by the Bering Sea.

WHERE IN THE WORLD?

Fossils have been discovered in North America, China, and North Africa.

HOW BIG IS IT?

JAW
Amebelodon's shovel-like lower jaw carried two huge teeth.

PREHISTORIC ANIMAL

TERTIARY (MIOCENE)

TIMELINE (millions of years ago)

| 540 | 505 | 438 | 408 | 360 | 280 | 248 | 208 | 146 | 65 | 1.8 to today |

Daeodon

• **ORDER** • Artiodactyla • **FAMILY** • Entelodontidae • **GENUS & SPECIES** • *Daeodon shoshonensis*

VITAL STATISTICS

FOSSIL LOCATION	Agate Springs Quarry, Nebraska
DIET	Probably omnivorous
PRONUNCIATION	DAY-oh-don
WEIGHT	2000 lb (907 kg)
LENGTH	11 ft (3.4 m)
HEIGHT	8 ft (2.4 m) at the shoulder
MEANING OF NAME	"Destructive tooth"

FOSSIL EVIDENCE

The massive bonebed at Agate Springs Quarry in Nebraska shows where dozens of *Daeodon* died together, most likely during a drought. Bones of the mammal *Moropus* have been found that seem to carry the tooth marks of the predatory *Daeodon*, which had the teeth of a savage hunter, although it also ate plants. Some paleontologists believe the "warts" on *Daeodon*'s skull may have been attached to the mammal's powerful jaw muscles.

PREHISTORIC ANIMAL

TERTIARY (MIOCENE)

The gigantic hoglike *Daeodon* was a tusked mammal, with huge jaws that could probably crush bones.

SPINE
Daeodon had a hump above its shoulders that was supported by the vertical bumps on its spine.

JAW
Bony "warts" along the lower jaw may have supported the mammal's powerful jaw muscles.

TEETH
The sturdy teeth of *Daeodon* at first seem like the teeth of carnivores, but certain details suggest they were omnivory— it may have also been a scavenger.

WHERE IN THE WORLD?

Fossils have been discovered in North America and East Asia.

HOW BIG IS IT?

TIMELINE (millions of years ago)

540	505	438	408	360	280	248	208	146	65	1.8 to today

Deinogalerix

• **ORDER** • Erinaceomorpha • **FAMILY** • Erinaceidae
• **GENUS & SPECIES** • Several species within the genus *Deinogalerix*

VITAL STATISTICS

FOSSIL LOCATION	Gervasio Quarry, Foggia Province, Apulia, southern Italy (Gargano Island during the Miocene)
DIET	Insectivorous/ carnivorous
PRONUNCIATION	die-no-ga-LEH-rix
WEIGHT	20 lb (9 kg)
LENGTH	24 in (60 cm)
HEIGHT	Unknown
MEANING OF NAME	Probably "terrible *Galerix*" because it was larger than, but similar to, the other fossil hedgehog *Galerix*, whose name, in turn, probably means "wearer of a skullcap"

Deinogalerix lived in what is now Italy around 11.2 million years ago, and belonged to the gymnures, or moonrat, family. But it was actually more like a hairy, giant hedgehog on long legs.

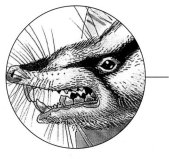

SKULL
One of the larger *Deinogalerix* species, *D. koenigswaldi*, had a skull 8 in (20 cm) long and a body 24 in (60 cm) in length.

FOSSIL EVIDENCE

First described in 1972, fossil finds show that the skull of *Deinogalerix*, with its thin, cone-shaped face, measured 8 in (20 cm) long, making up to one-third of its body length. This may have been an example of so-called island gigantism, a natural process by which creatures isolated on islands sometimes grow larger in size compared to those on the mainland. Unlike the modern hedgehog that it otherwise looks like, *Deinogalerix* had hairy skin instead of quills.

PREHISTORIC ANIMAL

TERTIARY (MIOCENE)

CLAWS
Deinogalerix likely used its fierce claws to catch the different things it ate, which could have included beetles, dragonflies, and crickets, as well as snails and lizards.

WHERE IN THE WORLD?

Fossils have been found in Italy.

HOW BIG IS IT?

TIMELINE (millions of years ago)

540	505	438	408	360	280	248	208	146	65	1.8 to today

Homalodotherium

• **ORDER** • Notoungulata • **FAMILY** • Homalodotheriidae
• **GENUS & SPECIES** • *Homalodotherium cunningham*

Homalodotherium, discovered in 1869, was one of the biggest of all the land mammals uncovered at Argentina's Santa Cruz Formation. It was well-adapted to the herbivorous life.

VITAL STATISTICS

Fossil Location	Santa Cruz Formation, Tarija Province, Argentina
Diet	Herbivorous
Pronunciation	Hoe-mallo-doh-THEH-rium
Weight	Unknown
Length	6 ft 7 in (2 m)
Height	Unknown
Meaning of name	Possibly "smooth-tooth beast"

FOSSIL EVIDENCE

Fossils of *Homalodotherium* showed that the mammal had short, stocky back legs and longer, flexible arms. One important feature of the fossil was an extremely large upper arm bone. This showed large ridges where strong muscles were attached when it was alive. This probably gave *Homalodotherium* extra strength for digging roots or pulling on branches. It walked along like a ground sloth, on the outside edge of its feet in a pigeon-toed fashion.

WHERE IN THE WORLD?

Remains were found at Santa Cruz Formation in Argentina.

JAW
Homalodotherium probably pulled down branches to feed on the leaves, just like today's giant pandas.

ARTICULATED WRIST
The flexible wrist likely helped *Homalodotherium* to grasp branches and pull them down so it could eat leaves and fruit.

HOW BIG IS IT?

PREHISTORIC ANIMAL

TERTIARY (MIOCENE)

TIMELINE (millions of years ago)

540	505	438	408	360	280	248	208	146	65	1.8 to today

Moropus

• **ORDER** • Perissodactyla • **FAMILY** • Chalicotheriidae • **GENUS & SPECIES** • Several species within the genus *Moropus*

VITAL STATISTICS

Fossil Location	United States
Diet	Herbivorous
Pronunciation	More-OH-puss
Weight	Unknown
Length	Unknown
Height	8 ft (26 m) at the shoulder
Meaning of name	"Sluggish foot" because it was thought to be a slow, clumsy mover

FOSSIL EVIDENCE

Moropus had short, sturdy back legs and longer, flexible front legs. It belonged to the group called chalicotheres, the same group of odd-toed mammals that today include horses, rhinoceroses, and tapirs. Its molars were broad and low, perfect for browsing on soft, leafy vegetation. It did not have horns or antlers to stop it from feeding from shrubs or thick trees.

WHERE IN THE WORLD?

Remains have been found at Agate Springs Quarry, Nebraska.

Moropus lived around 23.5 million years ago in North America. It was a strange-looking animal that looked like a horse with large claws.

NECK
A ball-and-socket arrangement in its neck vertebrae helped *Moropus* to hold its head unusually high when eating leaves.

HOW BIG IS IT?

FEET
Morophus was probably a selective browser and may have used its massive claws to dig for tubers.

PREHISTORIC ANIMAL

TERTIARY (MIOCENE)

TIMELINE (millions of years ago)

540	505	438	408	360	280	248	208	146	65	1.8 to today

Borophagus

• **ORDER** • Carnivora • **FAMILY** • Canidae • **GENUS & SPECIES** • Several species within the genus *Osteoborus*

VITAL STATISTICS

FOSSIL LOCATION	United States
DIET	Carnivorous
PRONUNCIATION	bor-oh-FAY-gus
WEIGHT	Unknown
LENGTH	Unknown
HEIGHT	2 ft (9 m)
MEANING OF NAME	"Devouring eater" because of its presumed ravenousness

Borophagus **was a prehistoric dog that lived in the United States around 6 million years ago, and looked a lot like a hyena. With its mighty jaws, it could probably crack and crush bone.**

NOSE
Like dogs today, *Borophagus* probably had a good sense of smell that helped it find the bodies of dead animals.

WHERE IN THE WORLD?

Fossils have been found at Edson Quarry in Kansas, Ogalalla Formation in Texas, and in Dixie County, Florida.

FOSSIL EVIDENCE

Borophagus was a primitive dog. It was probably a scavenger and ate the bones of the carcasses it found. Its teeth were shaped like cones and looked a lot like the teeth of the modern hyena. *Borophagus* was also characterized by a bulging forehead. Wandering the plains of North America, *Borophagus* probably used its sharp sense of smell to scavenge carcasses.

HOW BIG IS IT?

TEETH
Broad curved fangs at the front of the mouth were covered with thick enamel.

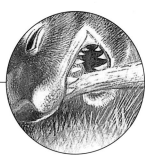

PREHISTORIC ANIMAL

TERTIARY (MIOCENE)

TIMELINE (millions of years ago)

540	505	438	408	360	280	248	208	146	65	1.8 to today

Syndyoceras

• **ORDER** • Artiodactyla • **FAMILY** • Protoceratidae • **GENUS & SPECIES** • *Syndyoceras cooki*

VITAL STATISTICS

FOSSIL LOCATION	United States
DIET	Herbivorous
PRONUNCIATION	Sin-die-AH-she-rass
WEIGHT	Unknown
LENGTH	5 ft (1.5 m)
HEIGHT	Unknown
MEANING OF NAME	"Together horn" because its snout horns are fused at the base

FOSSIL EVIDENCE

It looked like a deer, but *Syndyoceras* had more in common with the prehistoric camels. *Syndyoceras cooki* was first described by the paleontologist George Barbour in 1905. But it was 1968 before a remarkable collection of fossils was found hidden beneath the surface of Wildcat Ridge, Nebraska. Excavation started in earnest in 1999 under the University of Nebraska State Museum's Highway Salvage Paleontology Program. Among the 46 species discovered on Wildcat Ridge was an extremely rare *Syndyoceras*. It had teeth similar to present-day cattle and deer.

PREHISTORIC ANIMAL

TERTIARY (MIOCENE)

Syndyoceras looked like a deer, but with an interesting difference. On its head it had two horns, rather than antlers, but there was also a second pair, fused together, at the base of its snout.

SKIN
Syndyoceras's horns were likely covered with skin like the ossicones of giraffes.

HORNS
The two sets of horns were used for attracting a mate or for battling with other males for dominance.

HOOVES
Syndyoceras had deerlike hooves. Two vestigial outer toes on each foot did not touch the ground.

HOW BIG IS IT?

WHERE IN THE WORLD?

Fossils have been found at Wildcat Ridge, Nebraska.

TIMELINE (millions of years ago)

| 540 | 505 | 438 | 408 | 360 | 280 | 248 | 208 | 146 | 65 | 1.8 to today |

Megatherium

• **ORDER** • Pilosa • **FAMILY** • Megatheriidae • **GENUS & SPECIES** • Several species within the genus *Megatherium*

VITAL STATISTICS

FOSSIL LOCATION	South America
DIET	Herbivorous
PRONUNCIATION	Megga-thee-rium
WEIGHT	5 tons (5000 kg)
LENGTH	18 ft (5.4 m)
HEIGHT	20 ft (6 m) when standing on hind legs
MEANING OF NAME	"Great beast"

FOSSIL EVIDENCE

The first *Megatherium* fossil was found in Brazil in 1789 and showed that *Megatherium* had powerful jaws. It probably moved around slowly whether on all fours or on its hind legs. When standing up, *Megatherium* used its short tail to balance its body and was tall enough to reach leaves that grew in the upper branches of trees. *Megatherium* had peglike teeth and used its powerful cheek muscles to help grind down the vegetation it ate.

Modern sloths are not very large animals, but *Megatherium*, a ground sloth, was one of the largest mammals ever to walk the Earth. Standing on its hind legs, it was roughly twice the height of a present-day African bull elephant.

CLAWS
There were three hooked claws on each forelimb and five large claws on both back feet.

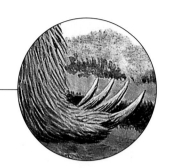

WHERE IN THE WORLD?

Megatherium originated in South America before migrating to North America.

HOW BIG IS IT?

GAIT
Because the huge curved claws on its toes got in the way, *Megatherium* walked on the sides of its feet.

TIMELINE (millions of years ago)

540	505	438	408	360	280	248	208	146	65	1.8 to today

Sivatherium

VITAL STATISTICS

FOSSIL LOCATION	India, southern Asia
DIET	Herbivorous
PRONUNCIATION	See-va-THEE-rium
WEIGHT	Unknown
LENGTH	Unknown
HEIGHT	7 ft (2.2 m) at the shoulder
MEANING OF NAME	"Beast of Shiva," after Shiva (considered the most important god in the Hindu religion,) since it was found in the Siwalik Hills of India

FOSSIL EVIDENCE

Its fossils are more commonly found in India. Despite its elk-like appearance, *Sivatherium* was a type of giraffe. Its shoulders were strong and heavily built to support the powerful neck muscles it needed to lift its heavy skull. The neck and limbs were relatively short and *Sivatherium* carried long, broad, flat horns on its head. The snout was wide, like that of a moose.

Sivatherium was an extinct type of giraffe. It probably looked like the modern okapi of Africa, but was much bigger.

OSSICONES
Sivatherium had two large ossicones (bony lumps) on its head and another, much smaller, pair above its eyes.

WHERE IN THE WORLD?

Remains have been found chiefly in India and around southern Asia.

HOW BIG IS IT?

BACK AND NECK
Some models of *Sivatherium* show a sloping back and a longer neck, though not as long as the modern giraffe's.

TIMELINE (millions of years ago)

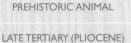

540	505	438	408	360	280	248	208	146	65	1.8 to today

Doedicurus

VITAL STATISTICS

FOSSIL LOCATION	North and South America
DIET	Herbivorous
PRONUNCIATION	Dee-dik-YOO-rus
WEIGHT	1.9 tons (2032 kg)
LENGTH	12 ft (3.6 m)
HEIGHT	5 ft (1.5 m)
MEANING OF NAME	"Pestle tail"

FOSSIL EVIDENCE

Doedicurus fossils are some of the most common mammal remains in the Argentingian pampas. *Doedicurus*'s armor was entirely rigid and it could not move as well as modern armadillos, who have a band of connected plates. The carapace on *Doedicurus*'s back was made up of large, thick osteoderms (plates made of bone). The tail was covered with a protective tube of bone that could have been up to 4 ft (1.3 m) long. Combined with the horny spines at the end, this was a strong weapon against predators.

PREHISTORIC ANIMAL

PLEISTOCENE

Doedicurus, a relative of the modern armadillo, lived during the Pleistocene Epoch until the close of the last Ice Age around 11,000 years ago. It carried an enormous domed shell on its back, which had many bony plates closely fitted together. *Doedicurus*'s head had a "carapace" (bony covering) of its own as a protection against attack. The tail had a covering of bone, ending in a club covered in sharp spikes. It lived in woodlands and grassland, which had plenty of plants and other vegetation.

WHERE IN THE WORLD?

Remains have been found in North and South America, particularly the Ensenada Formation in Argentina.

DENTAL PLAN

The teeth inside *Doedicurus*'s powerful jaws were a lot like the teeth of other herbivores. It didn't have teeth in the front of its mouth, but further back there were teeth used for grinding down the types of plants and leaves that grew in the grasslands and woodlands where it lived.

HOW BIG IS IT?

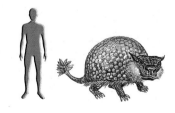

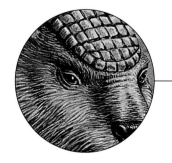

EYES
Doedicurus's eyes were tiny and had a limited field of vision.

• **ORDER** • Cingulata • **FAMILY** • Glyptodontidae • **GENUS & SPECIES** • *Doedicurus clavicaudatus*

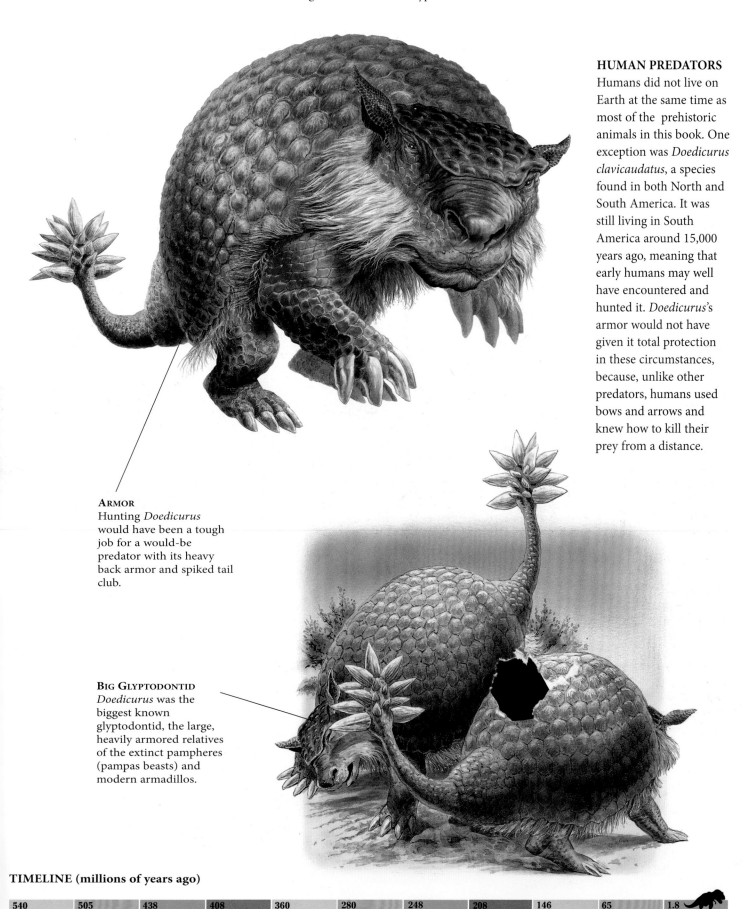

HUMAN PREDATORS
Humans did not live on Earth at the same time as most of the prehistoric animals in this book. One exception was *Doedicurus clavicaudatus*, a species found in both North and South America. It was still living in South America around 15,000 years ago, meaning that early humans may well have encountered and hunted it. *Doedicurus*'s armor would not have given it total protection in these circumstances, because, unlike other predators, humans used bows and arrows and knew how to kill their prey from a distance.

ARMOR
Hunting *Doedicurus* would have been a tough job for a would-be predator with its heavy back armor and spiked tail club.

BIG GLYPTODONTID
Doedicurus was the biggest known glyptodontid, the large, heavily armored relatives of the extinct pampheres (pampas beasts) and modern armadillos.

TIMELINE (millions of years ago)

540	505	438	408	360	280	248	208	146	65	1.8

Smilodon

VITAL STATISTICS

Fossil Location	The La Brea Tar Pits, Los Angeles; State of Minas Gerais, Brazil
Diet	Carnivorous
Pronunciation	SMILE-oh-don
Weight	220–884 lb (100–400 kg)
Length	19.7 ft (6 m)
Height	4 ft (1.2 m) at the shoulder
Meaning of name	"Chisel tooth"

FOSSIL EVIDENCE

The La Brea Tar Pits in Los Angeles, California, held hundreds of *Smilodon* fossils. They probably got stuck and died there while attempting to kill prey that had made the same mistake and also became trapped. This event gave paleontologists hundreds of complete *Smilodon* skeletons to study. Several finds were also made in South America in 1841 when a Danish paleontologist, Peter Wilhelm Lund, found fossils of *Smilodon populator* in caves in the state of Minas Gerais, Brazil.

PREHISTORIC ANIMAL

PLEISTOCENE

Smilodon was a big cat with a pair of long, sharp curved fangs. It is often popularly called a saber-toothed tiger, even though it is not closely related to the tiger. It was a very effective hunter and killer. To give greater effect to its hunting skills, *Smilodon* could open its mouth wide and position its fangs for the kill at an angle of 120 degrees. Its legs were very strong, and it could probably pull down large prey such as bison, elk, deer, mammoth, and mastodons.

FANGS
The extraordinarily long fangs could grow to a length of 7 in (17 cm).

HOW BIG IS IT?

WHERE IN THE WORLD?

Thousands of fossils have been found in tar pits and rocks from North and South America.

• **ORDER** • Carnivora • **FAMILY** • Felidae • **GENUS & SPECIES** • Several species within the genus *Smilodon*

FAT CATS

The earliest of the three *Smilodon* species officially recognized today was *Smilodon gracilis*, which lived around 2.5 million years ago. Weighing in at 221 lb (100 kg), it was the smallest of the species. *Smilodon fatalis* followed around 1.6 million years ago, living in both North America and western South America. *Smilodon fatalis* was a good deal larger and heavier, weighing up to 486 lb (220 kg). The third species, *Smilodon populator*, arrived 1 million years ago and was the largest of them all at 884 lb (400 kg).

AMERICAN ANIMAL
Smilodon lived in North and South America between 2.5 million and 10,000 years ago, co-existing with early human beings.

SEIZING PREY
Research in 2007 revealed how *Smilodon* probably killed its prey. Using the great strength of its upper body, it seized large victims and wrestled with them. It forced them to the ground and held them down while it used its fangs to stab through the large jugular veins. After that, *Smilodon's* prey bled to death very quickly.

HUNTERS
The fangs of both male and female *Smilodon* were usually about the same length, suggesting that both had roles as hunters.

TIMELINE (millions of years ago)

540	505	438	408	360	280	248	208	146	65	1.8

33

Smilodon

• **ORDER** • Carnivora • **FAMILY** • Felidae • **GENUS & SPECIES** • Several species within the genus *Smilodon*

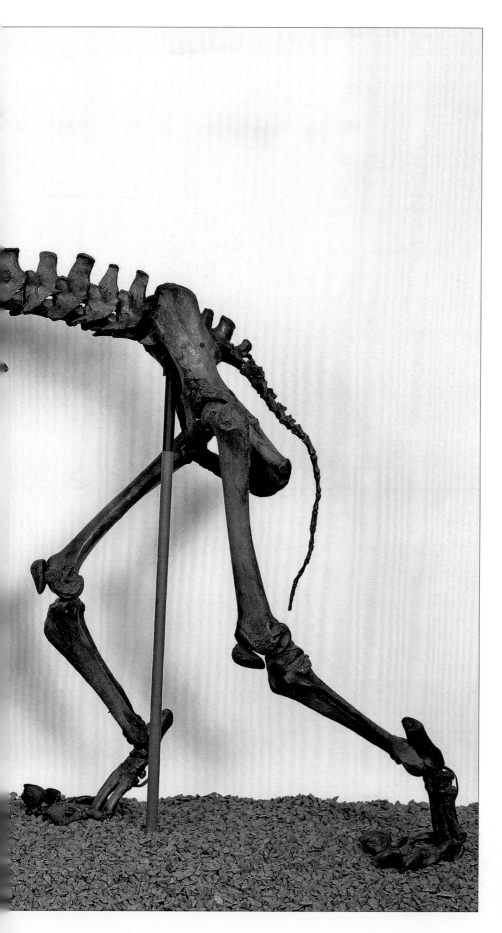

SMILODON FINDINGS

In 2007, a report published by the United States' National Academy of Sciences suggested that, despite its ferocious reputation, *Smilodon* was really something of a pussycat. First of all, the report claims, *Smilodon* did not belong to the same fierce species as tigers and lions. *Smilodon* could bite its victims only one-third as effectively as a lion. This was discovered when university paleontologists used fossils in a digital model of *Smilodon* and lion skulls. In computerized crash tests, *Smilodon's* skull and jaw failed to cope as long as the prey stayed on its feet and struggled to avoid death. In the same circumstances, though, the lion performed a great deal better and remained in control until the kill was completed. As one of the paleontologists, Colin McHenry of the UK's University of Newcastle, explained, "We simulated the forces you might expect if each one was taking large prey." This was not a matter of being better or worse though — what happened was evolution. *Smilodon*, it appears, had developed a weaker bite because of its small lower jaw, which had evolved to accommodate its long fangs.

Woolly Mammoth

VITAL STATISTICS

Fossil Location	Northern Hemisphere
Diet	Herbivorous
Pronunciation	WUH-lee MAM-uth
Weight	8 tons (8000 kg)
Length	25 ft (7.6 m)
Height	10 ft (3 m)
Meaning of Name	Possibly "Earth mole" after an imaginary underground animal from myths that emerges near rivers

FOSSIL EVIDENCE

Woolly mammoths are known from very abundant remains from the Northern Hemisphere. Some of the specimens found in the Siberian permafrost are famous for their wonderful preservation. Freezing preserves the skin, hair, eyes, viscera, muscles, gut contents, blood, parasites, and even DNA. Several examples of mummified baby woolly mammoths also exist; a recently discovered example promises to be the best-preserved fossil yet. It will be CT-scanned to reveal the internal organs, which are rarely studied for a long extinct species. Climate change has caused a lot of melting in Arctic environments, exposing more frozen remains.

PREHISTORIC ANIMAL

PLEISTOCENE

One of the most famous Ice Age beasts, the woolly mammoth is a widely recognized icon of the cold, and fairly recent, geological past. The woolly mammoth is just one of several mammoth species. It was a large relative of elephants that lived in cold climates and had a heavy coat of hair, as its name implies. Its skull had a more domed roof and its back sloped down toward the tail, whereas in modern elephants the back is more level.

DID YOU KNOW?
Woolly mammoths lived as recently as 4,000 years ago on Wrangle Island, north of Siberia. Most other mammoths became extinct 10,000 years ago.

HOW BIG IS IT?

TRUNK
Woolly mammoth trunks had two fleshy "fingers" at the tip that helped the animals grasp its food.

• **ORDER** • Proboscidea • **FAMILY** • Elephantidae • **GENUS & SPECIES** • *Mammuthus primigenius*

WHERE IN THE WORLD?

Woolly mammoths are known all over the Northern Hemisphere because colder climates were more widespread in the Pleistocene.

DID YOU KNOW?

Mammoths were once thought to be giant, underground burrowers that died when they accidentally broke through the surface and were exposed. This was a reason once offered to explain the weathering of the mummified remains.

FEET
Woolly mammoth feet had wide soles and a spongy pad that cushioned the weight of the animal's huge body.

MAMMOTH MEAL

A woolly mammoth is so huge that it would have been a huge task to cut up the carcass. Humans probably got around this by cooking the animal on the spot rather than trying to move it.

TIMELINE (millions of years ago)

540	505	438	408	360	280	248	208	146	65	1.8

Woolly Mammoth

• ORDER • Proboscidea **• FAMILY •** Elephantidae **• GENUS & SPECIES •** *Mammuthus primigenius*

TUNDRA MAMMOTH

The woolly mammoth, also known as the tundra mammoth, survived until around 1700BCE. This means it was one of the animals encountered and hunted by early humans. The woolly mammoth was also one of the first animals to have its picture painted. Prehistoric peoples painted the mammoth's picture on the walls of their caves in what is thought by some paleontologists to have been a ritual designed to ensure successful hunting. A huge elephant-like creature with curved tusks that could be up to 16 ft (5 m) long, the woolly mammoth was well protected against the intense cold in which it lived in the far north of North America and Eurasia and the frozen wastes of Siberia. Its shaggy coat was up to 35 in (90 cm) long, with a fine covering of wool for extra insulation next to its hide. The mammoth's ears were comparatively small at 12 in (30 cm) long, compared to the modern African elephant's, which measure 71 in (180 cm). But ears that were smaller meant that less surface area was exposed to the freezing temperatures. Under its skin, the woolly mammoth had a layer of fat up to 3 in (8 cm) thick, another characteristic that helped it to keep its body heat and keep warm.

Homotherium

• **ORDER** • Carnivora• **FAMILY** • Felidae • **GENUS & SPECIES** • Several species within the genus *Homotherium*

VITAL STATISTICS

FOSSIL LOCATION	North and South America, Eurasia, Africa
DIET	Carnivorous
PRONUNCIATION	Ho-mo-THEE-rium
WEIGHT	552.5 lb (250 kg)
LENGTH	5 ft (1.6 m)
HEIGHT	3 ft (1 m) at the shoulder
MEANING OF NAME	Either "man's beast" because the first fossils were found near human remains and artifacts, or "similar beast" for some unrecorded similarity

FOSSIL EVIDENCE

The fossil record shows that, like the present-day cheetah, *Homotherium* had an unusually large, square nasal opening. Also like the cheetah, the part of its brain that controlled sight was big and likely gave it extremely good sight both by day and night. However, the cat also resembled the hyena. Its front legs were long but its back legs were squat, making its back slope downward when it was standing. It may have hunted in packs to take down much larger animals.

PREHISTORIC ANIMAL

PLEISTOCENE

***Homotherium* was a so-called saber-toothed cat that lived between three million and 10,000 years ago.**

WHERE IN THE WORLD?

North and South America, Eurasia, Africa.

NASAL OPENING
Homotherium had an unusually large square nasal opening in its skull that probably helped it to breathe in more air, a valuable aid in pursuing prey.

HOW BIG IS IT?

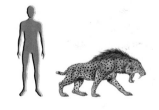

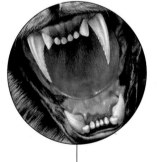

FANGS
Homotherium was a well-equipped killer with long, sharp fangs in its mouth.

TIMELINE (millions of years ago)

540	505	438	408	360	280	248	208	146	65	1.8

Coelodonta

• **ORDER** • Perissodactyla • **FAMILY** • Rhinocerotidae • **GENUS & SPECIES** • *Coelodonta antiquitatis*

VITAL STATISTICS

FOSSIL LOCATION	Ukraine, England, Belgium, Germany
DIET	Herbivorous
PRONUNCIATION	See-low-DON-tah
WEIGHT	3 tons (3000 kg)
LENGTH	11 ft (3.7 m)
HEIGHT	6 ft 6 in (2 m)
MEANING OF NAME	"Hollow tooth"

FOSSIL EVIDENCE

Coelodonta was among the megafauna (large animals) that lived during the last Ice Age, but became extinct around 10,000 years ago. *Coelodonta* first became known through paintings made by prehistoric hunters on the walls of their caves. The first fossil remains, however, were discovered buried in mud at Staruni, Ukraine. This find was a well-preserved female. Fossilized skulls of *Coelodonta* were also found in Germany and Belgium. Others were found frozen in ice or buried in earth saturated with oil.

PREHISTORIC ANIMAL

QUATERNARY

Coelodonta, the woolly rhinoceros, first appeared in Europe some 350,000 years ago, about halfway through the last Ice Age. They remained on Earth long enough to be hunted by early humans.

FRONT LIP
Coelodonta had a broad front lip that it used to cut down and eat plants.

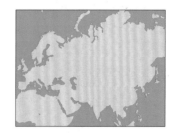

Fossils have been discovered throughout Europe and Asia.

FUR COAT
Heavy, shaggy fur protected *Coelodonta* against the cold temperatures of Ice Age Europe.

SKULL
Fossilized *Coelodonta* skulls have measured 30 in (76 cm) in length.

HOW BIG IS IT?

TIMELINE (millions of years ago)

540	505	438	408	360	280	248	208	146	65	1.8

Diprotodon

• **ORDER** • Diprotodontia • **FAMILY** • Diprotodontidae
• **GENUS & SPECIES** • Several species within the genus *Diprotodon*

VITAL STATISTICS

FOSSIL LOCATION	Australia
DIET	Herbivorous
PRONUNCIATION	Dip-roh-TOH-don
WEIGHT	6157 lb (2786 kg)
LENGTH	10 ft (3 m)
HEIGHT	6 ft (1.7 m) at the shoulder
MEANING OF NAME	"Two forward teeth"

FOSSIL EVIDENCE

The first *Diprotodon* fossils were found in a cave near Wellington, in New South Wales, early in the 1830s, and the next in Queensland about ten years later. Fossil finds showed that *Diprotodon*'s feet turned inward, and its footprints showed that they were covered with hair. Several finds seemed to show that death was brought on by drought. The mud of Lake Callabonna contained hundreds of *Diprotodon* that had died together. Their bodies were fairly intact, but their heads had been crushed. More than one female skeleton has been found with dead infants in its pouch.

PREHISTORIC ANIMAL

QUATERNARY

Diprotodon, who is related to modern wombats and koala bears, lived in the Australian forests, woodlands, and grasslands throughout most of the Pleistocene Epoch. They first appeared 1.6 million years ago.

CARING FOR YOUNG
Like many animals today, *Diprotodon* took great care of their young and taught them how to survive.

WHERE IN THE WORLD?

Remains have been found in New South Wales, Darling Downs, Queensland, and Lake Callabonna in Australia.

HOW BIG IS IT?

LARGE MARSUPIAL
Diprotodon was about the size of a modern hippopotamus. It was also the largest–known marsupial that ever lived on Earth.

TIMELINE (millions of years ago)

540	505	438	408	360	280	248	208	146	65	1.8

Glyptodon

• ORDER • Cingulata • FAMILY • Glyptodontidae • GENUS & SPECIES • Various species within the genus *Glyptodon*

VITAL STATISTICS

Fossil Location	North and South America
Diet	Herbivorous
Pronunciation	GLIP-toe-don
Weight	1 ton (1000 kg)
Length	6 ft (1.8 m)
Height	Unknown
Meaning of name	"Grooved or carved tooth"

Glyptodon was a large armored mammal, closely related to modern armadillos. The evident slowness of *Glyptodon* was not an enormous disadvantage for an animal so heavily armored from head to tail. It had a bony shell covering its back, which was made up of over 1,000 individual 1 inch (2.5 cm) thick osteoderms.

WHERE IN THE WORLD?

Many fossils of glyptodonts have been found in North and South America. They have helped to explain the movement of animals between these continents in the Pleistocene when Central America formed.

HEAD
Glyptodon was unable to withdraw its head into its shell. Its head was instead protected by a bony cap on the top of its skull.

FOSSIL EVIDENCE

Fossils of *Glyptodon* are common in the Pleistocene sediments of South America. The genus goes back to more than 1 million years ago and extends until about 10,000 years ago. Their fossils have been reported since at least the 1820s and are still plentiful. But human experience with these animals goes back much further than that; people had made it to the Americas thousands of years before *Glyptodon* became extinct and they would have been familiar with the living animal. The group to which *Glyptodon* belongs, the glyptodonts, made it to North America toward the end of the Pleistocene Epoch.

PREHISTORIC ANIMAL

QUATERNARY

HOW BIG IS IT?

SUPPORT
Glyptodon's body needed to adapt certain features to support its heavy body armor, such as short, massive limbs, a broad shoulder girdle, and fused vertebrae.

TIMELINE (millions of years ago)

540	505	438	408	360	280	248	208	146	65	1.8

Megaloceros
• **ORDER** • Artiodactyla • **FAMILY** • Cervidae • **GENUS & SPECIES** • Several species within the genus *Megaloceros*

VITAL STATISTICS

FOSSIL LOCATION	Europe, Asia
DIET	Herbivorous
PRONUNCIATION	MEG-uh-LAH-ser-us
WEIGHT	Varied
LENGTH	Varied
HEIGHT	6 ft 6 in (2 m) at the shoulder (Irish elk); 26 in (65 cm) at the shoulder (Cretan species)
MEANING OF NAME	"Great horn"

The most well-known species of *Megaloceros* is the Irish elk, which was very large and lived in open woods or meadows. Other species, from the Mediterranean, were much smaller.

FOSSIL EVIDENCE

There are nine recognized species of *Megaloceros*, the earliest being *M. obscurus*, which lived in Europe during the early Pleistocene. The many differences in the physical size of *Megaloceros* species are reflected in differences between their antlers. For example, *M. obscurus* had long, crooked antlers, whereas the antlers of *M. savini*, found in France, were straight, with prongs. *M. pachyosteus*, which lived in China and Japan, sported long, curved antlers. The most splendid antlers of all belonged to the Irish elk, or *M. giganteus*. Its antlers sprang from its head in broad, flat plates edged with pointed branches.

PREHISTORIC ANIMAL

QUATERNARY

ANTLERS
Potential mates would have been impressed by *Megaloceros*'s magnificent antlers. Equally, any male rivals would have been discouraged.

WHERE IN THE WORLD?

Remains have been found in Britain, Ireland, France, and Crete, as well as in China and Japan.

LEGS
Megaloceros had strong legs, which meant it could run from danger.

HOW BIG IS IT?

TIMELINE (millions of years ago)

540	505	438	408	360	280	248	208	146	65	1.8

Glossary

analogue (AN-uh-log) Something that is similar to something else

carapace (KAIR-uh-pays) A bony or shell-like covering on the back of an animal, like on a turtle

DNA (D-N-A) Short for deoxyribonucleic acid; acts as code in cells containing instructions for building genes

deciduous trees (dih-SID-ju-us) Trees that shed their leaves at some point in their life cycle

fossil (FAH-sil) Remains or traces of an organism from the past that have been preserved, such as bones, teeth, footprints, etc.

island gigantism (EYE-land jy-GAN-tizm) A process by which creatures isolated on an island grow larger than the same types of animals on the mainland

marsupials (mar-SU-pee-ulz) Mammals that carry their young in a pouch on their abdomen

ossicone (AH-sih-kown) Bony lumps

sagittal crest (SAH-ji-tul KREST) A bony ridge running down the middle of the skull

savannah (suh-VAH-nuh) A warm grassland with scattered trees

tapir (TAY-per) A modern mammal that looks closest to a pig

tusk (TUSK) A long, large tooth that can be used for digging or as a weapon

ungulate (UN-gyah-lit) A four-legged animal with hooves

vestigial (ves-TIJ-ee-ul) A small body part or organ that was more developed and useful on a creature's ancestors, but now has no use

Index

For More Information

Books

Holmes, Thom. *The Age of Mammals: The Oligocene & Miocene Epochs.* New York: Chelsea House Publications, 2008.

Lange, Ian. *Ice Age Mammals of North America: A Guide to the Big, the Hairy, and the Bizarre.* Missoula, MT: Mountain Press Publishing, 2002.

Turner, Alan. *National Geographic Prehistoric Mammals.* Des Moines, IA: National Geographic Children's Books, 2004.

Web Sites

To ensure the currency and safety of recommended Internet links, Windmill maintains and updates an online list of sites related to the subject of this book. To access this list of Web sites, please go to www.windmillbooks.com/weblinks and select this book's title.

For more great fiction and nonfiction, go to www.windmillbooks.com.